Family Guy™

Stewie's Guide to

WORLD DOMINATION

by Stewie Griffin

Helped into print by Steve Callaghan

Perennial Currents
An Imprint of HarperCollins*Publishers*

Dedicated to my trusted adviser, loyal friend,
and coffee-stained hand-me-down, Rupert
—S.G.

Dedicated to Beth, for all her love,
support, and laughter
—S.C.

FIRST EDITION

Designed by Timothy Shaner

Printed on acid-free paper

Library of Congress Cataloging-in-Publication Data

Callaghan, Steve, 1968–
    Family Guy: Stewie's guide to world domination/Steve Callaghan.
        p. cm.
    ISBN 0-06-077321-9 (pbk.)
        1. American wit and humor. I. Title

PN6165.C35 2005
818'.602—dc22   2004059927

05 06 07 08 09 ❖/RRD 10 9 8 7 6 5 4 3

The views represented in this book are mine, mine, mine, mine, mine. All mine. It was created solely for the purpose of entertainment. My entertainment mostly. (But, you know, if you get something out of it, too, I suppose I can't really do anything about that, now can I?) As a minor I take no responsibility whatsoever for what may happen if you are to follow my advice and actually dominate the world. Nor does the publisher, for that matter. Consider yourself forewarned (and rather pathetic, actually, for spending your valuable time reading all this legal poppycock instead of the book itself).

Contents

Contents

Contents

Introduction

Greetings, loyal minion. And thank you for purchasing the most useful guide you shall ever own. Well, except for *Who Moved My Cheese?* That thing knows what it's talking about. But I digress . . .

If you are holding this book in your hands, I assume that means you possess—as I do—a desire to rule as complete overlord whatever dominion you may have your eye on. It may be your sad, daily-grind of a drab workplace. It may be your precalculus class. Or, as in my case, it may be the entire free world.

But don't get ahead of yourself there, Paco. There's one essential fact you need to retain before you can ever hope to be as all-powerful as yours truly. And it is this: **The key to world domination is *understanding the world around you.*** To that end, I present to you, my loyal and obedient subject, this manual, which provides the foundation for that level of deep understanding. You may even think of it as a "Strategy Guide to Life."

So there it is. Now read on. Or if you're still thumbing through this tome in the bookstore, grow some 'nads for God's sake. Whip out that Discover card and pony up, man. I've got diapers to buy. All right, then.

Happy reading and burn in hell,

Stewie Griffin

Perhaps victory shall one day be yours, too.

Chapter 1

FAMILY, or My Case for Why I Surely Must Be Adopted

"Family" is one of those words that sounds harmless enough at first blush. Lord knows those Madison Avenue drones toss it about willy-nilly whenever it helps them sell more life insurance or toilet cleaner or Sunny Delight.

However, that term takes on a much more odious connotation in the case of someone such as myself, whose intellect far exceeds that of any of the other dullards occupying the same residence. You truly have no idea how tiresome it is to be the quickest wit in the bunch. I actually saw the fat man eating his deodorant the other day. That's right, dear reader. You heard me right. Eating his deodorant. This is precisely the reason why I have Social Services on speed dial.

In order to drive home the point about my daily suffering, I present to you as Exhibit A these thumbnail sketches of my fellow members of Clan Griffin. Read on, but only if you feel you have the stomach for it.

Hello, Social Services!

Paternity Test

POSITI

INCONCLUSIVE

PETER

Okay, let's talk genetics and evolution for a moment. You see, it was once explained to me that part of the universe's grand Darwinian plan included the notion that an infant should always bear a special resemblance to his father, lest he worry that some other bloke may actually be the father and therefore decide to eat the baby out of some sort of primal, competitive spite. In light of this premise, I respectfully offer one small inquiry as it pertains to my particular situation: "What the bloody hell?!"

Indeed, that dim-witted walking cautionary tale of heart disease and paint chip consumption could not be a more difficult individual with whom to live. He has dreadful taste in television and in women (clearly), and please do not get me started on the man's gas. I do apologize in advance to my more high-minded readers for delving into such a base topic, but I must get this one point off my chest: The man has ridiculously malodorous flatulence. We're talking toxic. And even worse, he appears to take a perverted delight in subjecting his other family members to his noxious fumes. It should be illegal. And you have no right whatsoever to judge me as one prone to hyperbole on this matter until you yourself have endured an evening with him postcabbage. You live through that twisted version of hell, then we'll talk.

My other beef with the man is his total lack of ambition. He wanders aimlessly from job to job like some dead-eyed drifter, barely pulling down enough to keep his offspring clothed and fed.

> The next one you can blame on the dog.

And dumb as a post he is. Oops, my apologies for sounding momentarily Yoda-esque there, but I trust you understand my point. The man needs instructions to find his navel. Hand to God, I once observed him opening a milk carton, and after mangling both sides, he literally cut it open with a bread knife. Staggering.

Well, I could go on and on about the corpulent simp, but there's so much more to say about the other nitwits, so I shan't linger here any longer . . .

I'm a bad father, a lousy husband, and a snappy dresser.

lois

Oh, dear. Where to even begin with this one? From the day this nefarious wench forced me through that cursed canal, I knew she had to be vanquished.

First of all, her condescending attitude is like nails on a chalkboard. "Are you ready for the airplane?" "Of course I'm ready for the damn airplane, you filthy skeez!" "Are someone's toofies hurting?" "They're called 'teeth,' you disgusting, swine-breathed vixen! Learn to speak the damn language!"

Yet despite her annoying manner, she must have nerves of steel and the stealth of a leopard. I have stopped keeping track of how many attempts on her life I have undertaken, only to be thwarted by her crafty moves.

And what in the bloody hell can you say about her choice of spouse? My best guess is that somebody humped somebody at the peak of drunkenness, forcing the traditional shotgun wedding—and, well, you know how the rest of that routine usually goes. I'm not saying that's definitely how it happened, but looking at the two of them, it's the

Damn you, vile woman! You've impeded my work since the day I escaped from your wretched womb!

best I can surmise. It's like one of those riddles that is never meant to be solved. Like crop circles. Or Bigfoot.

Anyhoo, some have questioned the reason for my matricidal tendencies. And it is an interesting question. I suppose those feelings ultimately stem from unresolved rage fueled by the cognitive dissonance created by the knowledge of my own intellectual superiority over her, juxtaposed with her simultaneous condescension and smugly false affection. Well, that or constipation.

Just down the hall from me is a room that houses the lovely Megan Griffin.

Good lord, is that girl a mess. Though to be fair, I wouldn't say it's entirely her fault. Sure, she needs a few pointers on fashion (here's one: Try not wearing the same hideous skullcap every day) as well as hygiene (here's another: Try not wearing the same hideous skullcap every day). **But what older female role models does the poor thing have around the house to emulate** in order to keep her from becoming the unsightly shrew she's evolving into? Well, you see my point.

Socially, the clumsy (well, I was going to say "waif," but that would be all wrong, wouldn't it?) lox hasn't the slightest clue. One Friday evening, I happened to peek in on her and found her alone in her room, lip-synching Christina Aguilera into her hairbrush. I couldn't help but look upon that scene and feel a certain sadness . . . for Christina Aguilera. Really, having her soul's work screeched out so arrhythmically by a person who is the very essence of all things decidedly not "Dirrty." Well, my heart goes out to the poor slut.

In the end, I suppose, my one true wish for Meg is that one day she might learn to throw like a girl.

> My one true wish for Meg is that one day she might learn to throw like a girl.

CHRIS

I've often said of Chris Griffin that he is as likely to enjoy *eating* a hot dog as he is *befriending* one. Not exactly Norman Mailer, this one.

However, the appeal of a simpleton such as Chris is obvious for a schemer such as myself. He's the perfect rube to execute my otherwise dangerous missions. And the perfect (though, often, unwitting) test subject. Why, just the other night, I laced his dinner with a truth serum I'm currently developing. Poor bastard spent the whole meal racing laps around the dinner table and shouting about wanting "boobie pudding" for dessert. Then he passed out in the garage for ninety-six hours. Kid soiled himself four times and nearly went into a coma. Just goes to show everything that comes out of R&D can't be a slam dunk right out of the gate.

Chris is presently a bit adrift as far as quality of life is concerned, and his future isn't looking as if it will become much brighter. Let's see . . . either he'll take after his father, packing on even more weight and shedding even more IQ points, or he'll take after his mother and become a total, raging bitch. Sadly, I fear all Chris has to look forward to is becoming one of those eccentric chaps one periodically sees on the local newscast who holes up in his studio apartment, having filled the entire place from floor to ceiling with old newspapers and rusty bikes.

> Oh, no, someone peed my pants.

You know those pack rat freaks I'm talking about, whose homes become so engulfed in detritus that they literally can't move. What's with those people? Seriously, if you come up with an answer, someone please e-mail me.

BRIAN

Ah, the dog. Thinks he's so brilliant, doesn't he? So aloof and holier-than-thou. That is, until someone turns on the vacuum and he urinates down his own leg and rushes for the nearest closet.

And he talks soooo much. Just shut the hell up for once! **I mean, we get it, you know?! You read** *The New Yorker.* Big whoop. So would most people if they didn't have a job and just sat around the house all day, taking periodic breaks to root through Lois's underwear drawer. That's right, I've seen him doing it and, frankly, it sickens me. I confronted him once and he claimed to be looking for his good sunglasses. Said he thought he might've set them down in Lois and the fat man's bedroom. But I think he knew I wasn't buying it. You know those tense moments where one person is lying and the other person knows he's lying, and the liar also knows

Oh, to be the Lindbergh baby now.

that the other person knows he's lying, but it's just too damn awkward, so we all just silently opt to move on and not acknowledge it? You've probably had a moment like that with your boss and his mistress, or your roommate and his long "showers." Anyway, it was like that.

At any rate, the mutt thinks he's so cool, but you know he's just a mess inside. Especially with women. **The most passably attractive woman saunters by, and out pops the "lipstick."** And then he prattles on like a giddy schoolgirl. It's truly disgusting to witness. One time when he was chatting up the salesgirl at Barnes & Noble, I literally vomited. Of course, Lois had given me some bad tuna earlier, but I'm quite certain it was the dog's clumsy and unseemly flirting that caused it. In fact, just thinking about it right this moment, I might have thrown up a bit in my mouth and swallowed it. *Yech.*

I just need a leg to hump.

The Rare Times When a Family Can Be of Some Use

1 Provides a convenient excuse for avoiding functions I'd rather not attend anyway. ("I'd love to come to the mud-pie potluck, but I've got this family thing . . .")

2 Lois's club store membership comes in handy for late-night trips to purchase car batteries in bulk (for fueling various nefarious devices).

3 Extra family members equals more presents at Christmas—one of which could turn out to be plutonium.

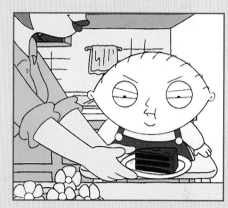

4 With six of us in the house, there is a birthday to celebrate every other month. (I may be evil, but it doesn't mean I don't like cake.)

5 When I send in the "12 CDs for a Penny" music club application, I can put Lois's name on it and, therefore, be off the hook when they come hounding me to buy more—and just leave it for her and the collection agency to hash out.

6 Thanks to the fat man's insistence on the most all-inclusive cable TV package, I can set TiVo season passes for *Queer Eye* and *Charlie Rose*.

7 There's always some dullard lurking about who can change my diaper.

Chapter 2

Love and the Sexes, or Why Women Are Such Confounding and Wicked Creatures

Some people have tried to suggest that I have a problem with women. I'd like to clear up that fallacy right now.

I only have a problem with redheaded, nasally voiced shrews who insist that I clean my plate at every meal. Truthfully, I don't care one bit that there are starving children in China or Africa or whatever other locale you care to toss around. That tidbit of info has no relevance whatsoever to the fact that my sweet potatoes taste like rhino dung.

That said, I've never understood the age-old struggle between men and women. Why make two models of people when one would do just as well and create fewer problems? I say, Henry Ford did quite well for a long time just by cranking out Model Ts, now, didn't he? And I know what you're thinking—the whole reproduction thing, hmm? Well, I would argue that if humans were to be made capable of asexual reproduction (like, for instance, those clever, clever spores) then there'd be no need for both sexes and we'd all be spared the trauma of sitting through hours and hours of bad stand-up comedy on why men and women differ so greatly (I'm looking at you, Rita Rudner).

I suppose what I'm saying is that God screwed up big time when he laid down the blueprints for humans. I'll give him the digestive system—amazing. The ability to heal oneself? Truly inspired. But the constant need for two sexes? He really crapped the bed on that one.

How to Handle Oneself with a Woman on One's First Date

Men have traditionally proven to be utterly clueless with regard to handling themselves when courting a young lady, particularly when first venturing out together to, say, the box social, or whatever the devil it is that kids are doing these days. Therefore, I humbly offer to you, dearest reader, these few guidelines for how to behave during your initial outing with a potential mate.

First, try to speak sternly and authoritatively. At least I always found such a tone to be most effective in dealing with Lois. Accordingly, when dining together, feel free to make liberal use of phrases such as, "Don't look at me, you hag!" and "You are not to begin eating until *I've* begun!"

Second, avoid cheesy colognes. Women want to smell your natural scent. In fact, evolution would dictate that your manly aroma is a powerful aphrodisiac. Therefore, taking this premise to its logical conclusion would advise that one should exercise vigorously

Don't look at me, you hag!

You must be a parking ticket, 'cause you got "fine" written all over you!

> When you do arrive to collect your lovely (or not so lovely, as the case may be) paramour, be sure to bring along a nice gift.

just prior to one's first date (preferably in a location with maximum temperature and minimal ventilation), but *under no circumstances should you then shower.* If you do so, you are essentially forfeiting one of nature's most potent tools for attracting Ms. Right.

And finally, when you do arrive to collect your lovely (or not so lovely, as the case may be) paramour, be sure to bring along a nice gift. Flowers are the traditional standard, of course, but in my learned assessment, they are not particularly useful or permanent. Indeed, those flowers on which you spent your hard-earned wages will be dead within a week. Instead, opt for something with greater usefulness and/or durability. Myself, I usually delight the lady with the thoughtful gift of stamps. They will always be useful and appreciated, for who among us is without a phone bill or cable bill crying out for the required postage? For that particularly special lady, I might wrap up and then present her with a handsome fire extinguisher. That thing'll last a lot longer than flowers, I'll tell you that right now—and it might even save her life (a surefire way to win a woman's heart).

So, there you have it. But I advise you to apply these rules with great care. What you have in your hand amounts to no less than the secret password for decoding the opposite sex. I only ask that you treat it with the reverence it deserves. And as that weird, decrepit fellow from *Hill Street Blues* used to say, "Let's be careful out there."

How to Tell If That Special Someone Likes You Back

Yo can be certain the feelings of affection are mutual if he/she

1 Makes admiring remarks about your collection of "Taft/Sherman in '08" buttons.

2 Offers to hold your hair back while you vomit from excessive alcohol intake (or an upset stomach caused by Children's Tylenol).

3 Always saves you an adjacent spot around the Gymboree parachute . . . but tries to pretend that it just worked out that way.

4 Is overly inquisitive about who is on your Friendster list.

5 Actually *volunteers* to change your diaper (even the back-loaded ones).

Most Romantic Ways to Propose to Your Lady

I s it time to finally succumb to the biological and social construct known as eternal matrimony? Well, if you happen to find that you've been appropriately brainwashed by that pervasive cultural myth of finding your one true love and you feel prepared to plunk down your hard-earned moola for that shiny rock on a brass ring, then here are a few gimmicks you might want to employ to make your "beloved" feel as though you've lived up to the ridiculous expectations that years of reading *Seventeen* have force-fed down her throat.

1 **Hire a gospel choir to sing your proposal.** This is always a good way to add a classy touch. And besides, the presence of strangers may make a fence-sitting mate reluctant to say no.

2 **Spell out your proposal in skywriting.** A bold choice. Just be prepared: Some courts may find that you are inadvertently entering into a written contract with every other woman in the county who happens to share your potential fiancée's name (i.e., *Marry Me, Sharon. Love, Gerald* will end up being read by *lots* of Sharons).

3 **Pop the question via the Jumbotron at the ballpark.** Always romantic, but if the response is a "no," this method carries the risk of your humiliation being replayed on the local jackass sportscaster's 11:00 P.M. blooper reel.

4 **Hide the engagement ring in her wineglass.** A classic, to be sure, but keep an eagle eye on that thing, lest you end up spending a stress-filled night in the ER having a diamond extracted from your sweetheart's pooper.

Chapter 3

Young People Today
<and Why They Need to
Shape Up or Ship Out>

Before I begin, I must say that I fully realize that each generation tends to believe that the level of corruption, immorality, and smut of the younger generation is worse than it has ever been. That having been said, young people today are a band of potty-mouthed, sex-crazed hooligans, all in desperate need of a kick in the pants and a day's worth of chores.

Let's begin with all the "street" behavior. I confess I am truly mystified that each and every time Lois drags me to the Stop & Shop we manage to run in to some gaggle of depressingly insecure Caucasian boys who feel they need to look and talk like African Americans. Do they think that's cool? Do they think it makes them more handsome

Fie on you!

Young people today are a band of potty-mouthed, sex-crazed hooligans, all in desperate need of a kick in the pants and a day's worth of chores.

to the fairer sex? Do they think it's going to garner the respect of their teachers, neighbors, and church leaders? Because, news flash: It's not going to do any of those things.

And you young ladies are no better. Why is it that every young woman I see on the street these days feels compelled at one point or another to screech out the latest pop ditty while using her hand to indicate the notes she thinks she's hitting, as if they were being registered on some imaginary musical scale adjacent to her head? I've got a breaking bulletin on this one, too: Just doing that thing with your hand doesn't make you sing on key, sister. At all. So, please, all of you Britney wanna-bes, a few less hand gestures, a few more voice lessons.

And, finally, what is with the obsession with sex? That's all you young people think about. If that's all you're focused on, then who among you is ever going to be the one to come up with the meaning of life or the cure for cancer or a piece of gum that keeps its flavor for more than six bloody seconds? This is how the world becomes a better place, young people— by stretching ourselves to the next level of science and literature, not by Googling the photos of the latest celebrity to have her boob accidentally pop out on stage. Oh, go on, get out of here. All of you. You all make me sick.

What the deuce are you staring at?

Why MTV Is the Root of All Evil

Now, I realize how fond all the young people are of MTV (and MTV2 and MTV Latino, or whatever the hell other channels those jackasses are running these days), but I must tell you, those people are propagating nothing but pure evil and moral decay. A few pieces of evidence to bolster my argument:

1 There's no bloody music on the network anymore! Yes, I'm aware this is an age-old complaint, but the word "music" is right there in the name of the channel, you loathsome cretins. At the very least, stop being disingenuous and just go ahead and change the name of the network from MTV to *Road Rules-Pimp My Ride*-and-Intoxicated-College-Students-Doing-Disgusting-Stunts-for-No-Pay-but-Rather-Because-Someone-Shoved-a-Camera-in-Their-Faces TV.

2 MTV's advertising does nothing but convince our young men and women that their faces are too filled with acne, their armpits are too foul-smelling, and their tampons are not absorbent enough . . . when it should instead be instructing them to worship and follow *me*!

3 *The Real World* is *still* on?! Really?! Really?! I mean, come on, hadn't we all gotten our fill of insipid, totally staged pseudoconflict back in, say, I don't know, 1991?

> Ha! That's so funny, I forgot to laugh—excluding that first "ha."

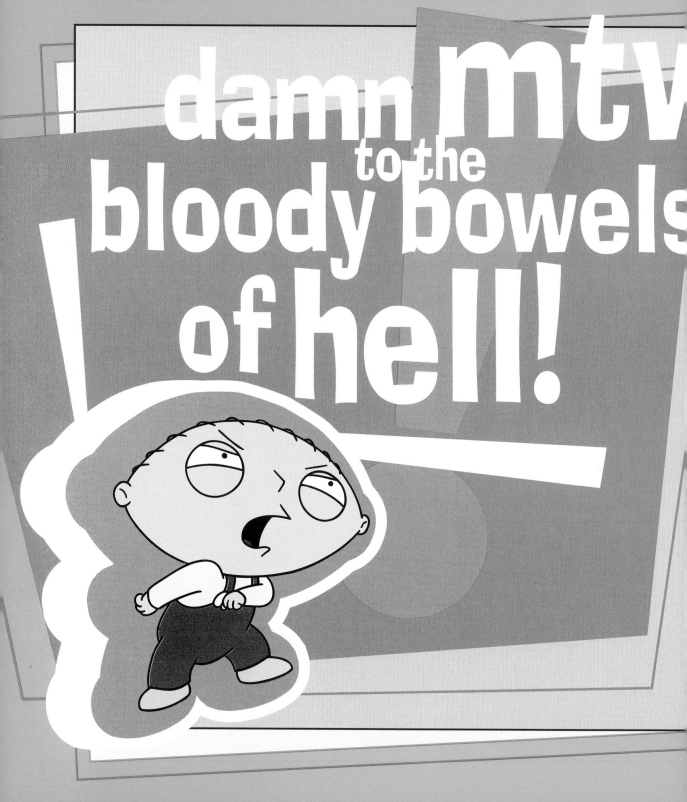

4 A word about *Punk'd:* This is the best we can do? Pulling vicious pranks on people and then watching them try not to throw a punch at someone? (Okay, I confess I must come a little clean on this one, because there was, in fact, one episode that did give me a chuckle . . . Tracy Morgan screaming and cursing at that chap who towed his car. Oh, please, I filled an entire Huggies on that one.)

5 And "Wildboyz"? Is that supposed to be cool? Are we supposed to feel that the "boyz" in question are particularly "wild" because of the crazy and utterly incorrect Z at the end of the word? Pay attention, people. This is precisely why the United States is the second dumbest nation on the planet. *Aaaugh!*

6 I'm fairly certain I would rather pound my own skull repeatedly into the wall for thirty minutes than sit through the televised adventures of Jessica Simpson picking out nail polish with her pea-brained friends.

Enough with the
Childhood Obesity Already

All right, young people, pull up a chair. There is a matter of grave concern that we must discuss. And here it is: For the love of God, put down the Xbox controller and get off your bloody ass!

That's right, step outside once in a while! Ride a bicycle! Chase a hoop with a stick down a dirt road! Whatever the devil you kids are doing these days, do some of *that*! For God's sake, the epidemic of childhood obesity in this country has reached absurd proportions. Not only is it terribly unhealthy for you, but, quite frankly, you're disgusting to look at whenever I have the misfortune of having to stare at your oozing guts in the mall, or the market, or the hardware shop.

But it really is even bigger than that, young people. Collectively, all you Fatty Fattersons are making us look like imbeciles on the world stage. Look around you—at France, Pakistan, the Sudan—honestly, at any other bloody country but our own. Do you see hordes of fat children running amok like you do in these fifty states? The answer, in case you were too busy gulping down your McDLT and Shamrock Shake to hear the question, is NO! So, stop embarrassing us in front of the other nations of the world! You're sending the message that we're too dumb to know any better than to shut our pieholes once our pants have stopped

RUE the day!

fitting us properly. And once they stop respecting us, they're certainly not going to come to our aid in any sort of international situation where we may want their help.

So, if you remember nothing at all of what I've said here, remember this: Each beef chimichanga you mindlessly wolf down is a small victory for the terrorists. Now go back to the saturated fat-filled, oversize portion I'm sure the Chili's waitress just plopped down in front of you. I can see I'm fighting a losing battle here.

Each beef chimichanga you mindlessly wolf down is a small victory for the terrorists.

Teen Fashion Horrors

Now I'm as aware as the next fellow of the capriciousness of teen fashion. However, I'd like to offer some advice to you young men and young women out there who think you are upholding your adolescent duty to conform by looking like you do.

For the Young Men

■ Not all of you are (or need to be) skateboarders.

■ Cut that ridiculous mop-top head of hair. (That's right. I said you look ridiculous.)

■ Pull up those pants. No one wants to see your underwear, least of all yours truly.

■ Wipe that stupid smirk off your face before I blast it off for you.

For the Young Ladies

■ You look like a slut. Stop dressing like one.

■ No one thinks your decision to spear your navel with a belly ring makes you look grown-up. Even less so if infection sets in.

■ Stop taking your cues from those trollops you see in the moving pictures and on TV. Not everyone's chest can look like Lindsay Lohan's (without surgery, that is).

■ And, ladies, cover up those cracks. Enough said.

Stop taking your cues from those trollops you see in the moving pictures and on TV.

FOR GOD'S SAKE,
GET OFF YOUR ASS
AND DO SOME PARENTING!

Chapter 4

Parenting <and I'm Not Referring to Any of This "Time-out" Nonsense>

I'm not altogether confident that I truly have much to offer on this subject, but then I look at someone like Ozzy Osbourne. For God's sake, that fellow is so clearly ill-equipped to father anything and yet he's somehow managed to keep those kids alive (well, for now anyway). By the way, Ozzy, if you happen to be reading this: What the hell happened, man? You used to be the prince of frigging darkness and now you're just some doddering pathetic joke who can't keep his kids in line or his pets from crapping on his Persian rugs. Pull it together, buddy, and start cracking some skulls around that place.

In any event, if Mr. Osbourne can purport to offer insight on the subject of parenting, then I suppose I can certainly take a whack at it. However, my observations will of course attempt to illuminate the topic of parenting from the perspective of one who is parented on a daily basis and, therefore, can speak to the techniques that result in a contented child and those that make the child want to perform acts of matricide (the latter category being the far larger of the two).

So, You Think You Want to Become a Parent, Do You?

So, you're ready to take the plunge, eh? Thinking about blending your gametes with that special (or more likely, that mildly impressive, nothing-to-really-write-home-about-but-occupying-a-semilucrative-middle-management-position-with-breath-that's-not-completely-heinous) someone? Then you've come to the right place.

Adding another human to the planet is no small undertaking. You should plan on having your life changed forever. In that spirit, I present to you a likely scenario of a day in the life of a new parent (based entirely, of course, on my own firsthand knowledge of the child end of the equation). So, read on, prospective parent. But you may want to sit down first.

4:27 A.M. My alarm goes off so I can rise and let loose my loudest, most theatrical cry, in order to wake that horrid, redheaded beast. I do this because I know her well enough to know that once she's awake, it's nearly impossible for her to fall back to sleep. Take note, reader: Sleep deprivation can be a powerful tool against your enemies.

6:03 A.M. Suckle some of that rancid milk from that dilapidated teat. Makes me look like a rube, I realize, but a fellow has to eat, no?

6:05 A.M. Crap myself. Not because I have to; just to keep her on her toes, show her who's boss.

7:10 A.M. Hurl my breakfast across the room. This week, I've decided to go for a new distance record.

9:29 A.M. Get schlepped to the grocery store. Punish the wench for intruding on my busy schedule by faking a tantrum over every stupid trinket at the check-out counter. Do you know that I nearly got her to buy me a disposable camera last time? Weak, weak woman.

11:45 A.M. Get dragged around even more. This time to swim lessons with Darrin, a hopeless drip of a person who's "still taking classes at the junior college while he crashes with his parents for a while longer." The fellow is thirty-four.

12:58 P.M. Have the White Trash lunch of cheese, bread, and yogurt crammed down my throat while I sit restrained by actual straps. Abu Ghraib would be a step up from this treatment.

2:10 P.M. "Nap time," which I actually use to download blueprints from the Web and check e-mail.

4:41 P.M. Get dragged around once more, this time to the park. Restrained (again) in a swing and flung about in a repetitive motion, not unlike a pendulum. I actually use this as my meditation time. Center the ol' chakras and such, you know.

5:20 P.M. Throw a screaming tantrum for no reason at all. Ha!

6:01 P.M. Dinner. More cheese. Seriously, are you trying to give me a bloody heart attack, bitch?

6:40 P.M. Watch *Baby Einstein* video. You know, honestly, the thing is damn entertaining. I just wish that woman who created them—and who insists on featuring her daughters in every one of the things—would figure out that *no one* thinks her kids are as adorable as she apparently does. In fact, the elder one is downright irritating, what with her affected manner and smug smiles. Just some feedback, Julie, that's all.

7:01 P.M. Bath. On a good night, I'll actually pee on Lois. Nothing funnier.

7:45 P.M. Off to bed. Although, truth be told, I usually stay up until around 11:30, working on devices or plans. Or on Thursdays, maybe I'll sneak in *CSI*. Jorja Fox. Me-ow.

So there you have it. My point is, it's exhausting. So, read this over before you decide to do the nasty with that suitor of yours who's been jonesing to get in those pants. It just might be the most effective birth control you could own.

Actual Parenting Techniques from the Nineteenth Century That May or May Not Need to Make a Comeback

I f you find your children griping to you about how badly you mistreat them, feel free to share with them some of the following examples of actual parenting techniques from the nineteenth century. While I would be truly evil to say that I felt some of them should make a comeback, one can't help but think that perhaps—just perhaps—some current parenting methods get shuffled aside before it becomes truly necessary to do so.

And without further ado . . .

1 Per John Locke (a well-regarded expert on such matters way back when), children should be dipped in ice cold water five times a day in order to keep them from getting too soft or civilized by warmth and comfort.

2 Locke also believed that children should remain barefoot at all times.

3 To discourage children from crawling (an activity regarded as animalistic), other such experts advised parents to bundle and tightly swathe children in cloth. This led some adults to play a form of football with the wee things.

4 And, finally, to keep children from pleasuring themselves, parents were advised to make them sleep in metal mitts or with their hands tied to the bed.

Ah, progress. But then, who's to say? Perhaps Darwin did some of his best thinking while being dunked in ice cold water. After all, one can't help but wonder if we'd have landed a man on Jupiter by now if only there were a few more children in metal mitts.

Signs That Your Child Is Trying to Kill You

Are you absolutely certain you are not being targeted by your otherwise sweet and cheery offspring? Don't be so sure. That nasal-voiced dullard certainly seems to have no clue I'm gunning for her. May I suggest you look for these warning signs:

1 You discover unexplained puncture marks in your furniture. And you don't own a cat.

2 You notice brake fluid mysteriously pooling under your brand-new car's front end.

3 That C-sharp on your piano hasn't worked in weeks. When you check it out, you notice the wire for that key is missing.

4 You spy a strange trail of dead insects leading to the trash where you tossed out your lunch because "it tasted funny."

5 Your child insists that you watch *According to Jim* together. I kid, of course; that would only make your eyes bleed.

Chapter 5

Difficulties of Being a Baby, or Why Teething Is Not for the Faint of Heart

It may sound like bragging, but **I must say that I've done quite well for myself, particularly given my small stature and fairly limited bowel control.** And, of course, there are many advantages to being the infant I am (smaller hands can more easily manipulate the technical wiring found in many spy-cams and remote control detonators, for instance). However, a baby has many more limitations than one might at first realize. In this section, I shall explore some of the oft-neglected downsides of being at a stage when waving "bye-bye" is regarded by those around you as a major achievement.

Oh, and by the way, I had such fun in the last chapter directing my comments personally to Ozzy Osbourne that I thought I'd similarly indulge myself here, only this time to Mr. Jimmy Fallon. So, here we go. Oh, hey there, Jimmy. How are you? What's going on? Nice haircut, bro. Oh, hey, I got a message here for you. . . . Yeah, that amateurish breaking of character and staring at the camera thing you do? No one but Horatio thinks that's funny, you twit. Besides which, it's totally unprofessional. There, I said it. Now you may go back to making *Taxi 2: Electric Boogaloo* or whatever the hell it is you were up to.

My most sincere apologies to you, dear reader, for that digression, but I hope you would agree that it simply had to be done. Now then, please read on . . .

Teething

When was the last time you burned yourself on . . . oh, I don't know, let's say some soup that was perhaps a scosche too hot? Quite painful, isn't it? Well, imagine that pain in your mouth extended over a period of many long months, multiply it times twenty, then imagine that that seafood gumbo is actually an iron rod being rammed through a pinhole by a team of rabid oxen. Okay, now that's *one* tooth.

Again, I give much props to the man upstairs for his other numerous designs. The oceans, a sunset, Jennifer Garner—all amazing specimens. But if this whole "you're not born with teeth, they have to move painfully and individually into place" thing crossed someone's desk at the R&D department at any of the major Fortune 500 companies, the person who created that design would be looking for a job faster than you can say "faster than you can say." (You see what I did there? Sometimes I even tickle myself.)

So, every few weeks, I'm left to writhe around in my crib all night in searing pain because somebody in the Big Man's factory wanted to go home early to watch *Monday Night Football*. And to make matters worse, that horrid shrew refuses to give me any pain medication whatsoever to alleviate the torture I'm enduring. No, not even a frigging Tylenol!

Now, I know what you're saying, and believe me, you're preaching to the choir on this one. But, apparently, the woman read some homeopathic/holistic healing garbage in her *Shape* magazine and now I'm the one who has to pay the price so that she can feel good about herself, even though she wolfs down a gargantuan bowl of ice cream every night before bed. Yeah, that's not hypocritical at all.

I suppose what I'm driving at here is, when it comes to teething pain, for the love of God, say yes to drugs.

The outrages I've suffered today will not soon be forgotten!

Having to Feign Amusement at Stories of the Tooth Fairy

Another significant downside of being my age is the responsibility foisted upon me to remain complicit in this whole Tooth Fairy nonsense. Perhaps it's just in my nature to want to maintain the homeostasis of this giant cultural fraud (what can I say, I'm a people-pleaser!), but when you think about it, what choice do I really have? You see, **if I were to confess to knowing that the entire enterprise is a sham, then that delicious stream of cold, hard cash that appears under my pillow following the loss of a tooth gets suddenly cut off, doesn't it?** I mean, c'mon, man, I'm not stupid. Even I, Stewie Griffin, have bills to pay.

So, where does that leave me then? Having to pretend that I'm either so gullible or brain-dead as to actually believe that there exists a mystical fairy somewhere out there who is aware of every child who loses a tooth on a daily basis (imagine the bookkeeping that would require!) and also has the time and the necessary transportation to deliver him (or her, lest you think I'm even the slightest bit sexist) hither and yon simply to leave a few measly coins under each of the little brats' heads.

Okay, so fine, fine. Let's just say we shut off all reasoning skills for the moment and assume that this fairy has a seemingly endless supply of spare change (from where, by the way? Digging through people's trash for recyclables?), not to mention the interest in performing this rather tedious function. My question, then, is WHAT HAPPENS TO ALL THE TEETH? With a world population of 6 billion people, let's say that 2 percent of them are within teeth-losing age; that's 120 million children. And let's say that just 1 percent of them are losing their teeth in any given *month*, well, now we're still talking about 1.2 million teeth per month!

You see my point. How utterly absurd, then, that someone as brilliant as myself should have to go along with such a horrendous fraud! Frankly, I find it all just too frustrating to think about any longer, so I'm going to retire to my room now to do what I always do when I need to relax: write my wish list for Santa.

Chapter 6

School/Preschool, or This Excuse for an Educational System We Have

Now, perhaps you might be thinking, "What right does a mere infant (who has never even set foot in a classroom) have to criticize the public school system in this country of ours?" To which I would ask back to you, in turn, dear reader: "How truly different is it for me to do so than for any of the endless line of policymakers who purport to know what's best for our schools when they themselves have been nowhere near a classroom since the days of the Johnson Administration?" **Ha! Take that, all you stuffy, out-of-touch politicians!** (By the way, that tiny cheer you may have just heard was the sound of the Teachers' Union engaging themselves in a collective, coast-to-coast "You go, girl!") But, anyhoo . . .

Now that I've gotten that off my chest, I'd like to offer my take on schooling today. Yes, I realize that the pastoral days of the one-room

EIGHTH GRADE IS FRIGGIN' CRAP!

schoolhouse are long gone, but surely there must be some happy medium between being spanked with a ruler for misbehaving in plowing class and having to be frisked by that malodorous rent-a-cop after you pass through the metal detector on your way to PE.

So, in the next few pages I hope to offer some information that might be useful to you as you make your way from those first scary days of kindergarten through your last bout of senioritis (a condition for which I recently invented a cure—it's called, "You better bring up that C average, Fatty, or it's off to the marines for you . . . and the Iraqis don't care how many letters you earned in water polo or how drunk you were the day of the SAT, got it?"). So, read on, won't you?

> Permission to freak out?

The "Three Rs"

And so as we begin our journey toward rooting out the causes of the decline in this country's educational standards, it appears that we need to look no further than the all-too-familiar bedrock educational principle of the "Three Rs."

Now let's examine this concept for a moment. Of course, we all know that the first of the three Rs is reading. Fine. No problem. I certainly can't argue with the importance of establishing a solid base of literacy and familiarity with the canon's great works of fiction and nonfiction. (Yes, even the overrated Faulkner. Okay, we get it, Bill, you can write like a retarded person. Kudos.)

But then we move on to the second of the three Rs: writing. Hmm. Does anyone else notice what I'm seeing? Here we are asking our young people to put writing in the top trio of their educational priorities, yet we cannot even be bothered to know what letter the damn word begins with! (Again, I blame the cursed MTV, but I digress . . .)

Then just when you think things can't get even a trifle more insulting, up sneaks the third R: 'rithmetic. That's right: 'rithmetic. Good lord, who invented these "Three Rs" anyway? Boss Hogg? Honestly, what learned person speaks like that? (And don't you dare say people from the South, because trying to make the case that there are learned people from the South is like trying to say that there are unicorns and leprechauns in Atlantis—that is, despite your childishly eternal optimism, it just comes off sounding like utter fantasy.)

So, if I've been paying attention, what we are left with is not the "Three Rs," but rather the R, the W, and the A. And in that case, why not form them into some clever acronym that would be just as easy to recall as the bloody "Three Rs"?

R. R. R.
W. A. R.!

For instance, there's no country that likes "W.A.R." more than our own. We like to wage it, watch it from a distance on television, then romanticize it on the History Channel for decades into the future. That could be a memorable acronym. Or how about "R.A.W."? I think you might agree that one has a certain lurid suggestiveness that is the very bread and butter of this country's conflicted moral psyche.

So, when one begins to look for the origins of our dilapidated school system, don't blame the children (at least not right away; I'll have some words about them in other parts of this tome), but rather blame the Boss Hoggs of the world who got the whole enterprise off on the wrong foot with this "Three Rs" nonsense. Although if you did want to try to blame them, I suppose you'd have to send a note by Pony Express or some damn thing since those bumpkins surely don't own any of today's newfangled devices.

If I Ran the School System

Iit's one thing, of course, to criticize the status quo, but quite another to actually put forward one's own vision of how one might do things differently. Therefore, allow me to articulate how I might endeavor to get our wretched mess of an educational system back on the right track.

First, no more PE. What the hell is PE, anyway? I mean, whose idea was it to throw away valuable learning time by doing chin-ups and playing Greek dodgeball? Work up a sweat on your own time, people. We can't be pissing away precious hours that could and should be spent on things like learning world history and memorizing how to disassemble a vintage crossbow.

Next, every child needs to wear a uniform. Not to minimize competitiveness in adolescent fashions, mind you, but rather just because I want to debase the entire student body by forcing them to wear drab, feces-covered jumpsuits (in order to make sure they know who's running things, you know . . .).

Another requirement of my system: no cafeteria. Who ever said it was the school's responsibility to educate the children and feed them, too? Nonsense. Eat before you come to school and bring a snack. I'm partial to those Fruit Roll-Ups, myself. (They're fun to peel and they sort of melt in your mouth. Hmm, I might have to go grab one right now, in fact. Back in a flash.) Okay, I'm back now.

No English class shall teach any literature from the twentieth century.
That's when we all got soft as a society, so those are most certainly not values
we want to be passing on to the up-and-coming generation. So, F. Scott
Fitzgerald, take your decadent little tales of adultery and obscene wealth, pack
them away in a trunk, and drop them in the bottom of the pool with your
beloved and very dead Gatsby. And fie on you, too, J. D. Salinger, although the
chances of you actually reading this are probably equal to the chances of you
stepping out of doors or using electricity.

And, finally, no lockers for anyone. Not only do the damn things smell hor-
rible when you open them, but as it is, they really
serve little purpose other than as a place to
lock up the nonalpha males in a bizarre
hazing ritual. And by forcing school children to lug around all their academic
materials, it may actually
teach them a bit of disci-
pline and cause them to
work up a bit of a sweat.
And, now that I think
of it, there's your
damn PE . . . hmm?

So, there you have
it. A school system under
the supervision of Stewie Griffin might
not be a particularly mirthful place, but at
least it won't produce the lazy, undisciplined
(and frankly, dunderheaded) citizens that our
current system is all too content to crap out.

The Great Gatsby

Everything I Ever Needed to Know I Learned in Preschool

A few months back, there was a period of several weeks when Lois felt she needed to discover herself, or just have a Calgon moment, or . . . well, quite frankly I don't know what the hell was going on in that presumably vacant cranium. But this was the brief interval when she actually enrolled me in a preschool program. That is, until I went out of my way to appear to be such a "disciplinary problem" that the teachers at the school refused to keep me there any longer. Don't worry, it was just a little clay-throwing and hair-pulling incident; I certainly didn't get McMartin on them or anything . . . yet.

In any event, with only slight apologies to the insipid scribblings of Robert Fulghum, I present the following list of things I learned from that brief period in my life, when my 8:00 A.M.s to 1:00 P.M.s meant sharing space with a room full of filthy, virus-carrying urchins.

1 Apparently most infants do not carry their own monogrammed handkerchief as I do. Nor would they have the slightest idea what to do with one if they did. What I'm getting at is, cover your bloody mouths when you sneeze, folks!

2 Crayons should not be scented to smell like food. Just ask Jeremy or anyone on the emergency room staff at Quahog General.

3 There is nothing fun about finger painting. Especially when you are paired with the ADHD kid.

4 Miss Karen and Miss Tanya need to spend a little less time on their smoke breaks and a little more time wiping down the disgusting, germ-laced nap mats. And finally . . .

5 If you trace your hand, it looks like a turkey!

Chapter 7

Work <and How I Intend to Avoid It>

I'm not really sure what I could say here that wasn't already flawlessly covered in the 1980 masterpiece *Nine to Five*, starring the always-hilarious Lily Tomlin, the mind-bogglingly endowed Dolly Parton, and former exercise guru and trophy wife Jane Fonda. That having been said, I shall attempt to impart to you here what I perceive as the unending conflict between the simultaneous need for a sturdy labor force to insure continued economic stability and the powerful individual desire to sit on one's keister all day.

As long as there has been a requirement to hold a job as a means of making a living, there have been people who have sought to avoid having to do so. And those individuals have traditionally fallen into two distinct camps: the clever and the purely lazy.

Now, the purely lazy do manage to avoid work, however they might typically lie about the house day in and day out fraudulently collecting disability checks while existing on little more than a steady diet of canned meat products and reruns of *Texas Justice*.

In stark contrast, those who seek to shirk work in a more clever manner usually do so with the assistance of that "one great idea" (e.g., the fellow who fooled us all into buying pet rocks a few years back) and are then able to spend their remaining days sipping champagne and bragging to moderately interested busboys about how they were the genius who invented the pet rock. Not the most charmed life, I'll grant you, but still a step up from slogging it out every day at the Arby's beef slicer for minimum wage.

> I got an idea . . . an idea so smart, my head would explode if I even began to know what I was talking about.

My Recommendations for Getting Rich Quick

Often, when one encounters the phrase "get rich quick," the other word that comes to mind is "scheme." However, you may rest assured that none of the ideas I've articulated below involves anything illegal or even remotely unethical (well, except for maybe four or five of them). Nonetheless, read on, if you would like to enjoy the trappings of the rich and famous without any of that pesky hard work.

1 Once a day, drive past your local recycling center and surreptitiously load your car with approximately 2,500 aluminum cans. Then, drive around to the front and redeem them once again for their full value. That's true recycling, no?

2 Create a phony, prop brick out of lightweight foam. Put a clever label on it, instructing the purchaser to use the brick as a cathartic, stress-reduction device by throwing it at the television when the referee makes a bad call during a favorite sporting event, etc. I guarantee you Spencer Gifts will lap that steaming pile right up.

3 Find your most gullible friend. Tell him that you'll pay him $100 if he'll just give you one penny. But then he has to double it and give you two pennies the following day, then double that to four pennies the next day, etc., but only for one month. (Do the math, genius, you'll see what I'm talking about . . .)

4 This is one I've actually done: Become so charming that people will pay you just for the pleasure of your company. And I know what you're thinking, but, no, this most certainly does not make me a whore. (Note: For those of you who are personality-impaired, I suggest you consider attending one of those silly courses at The Learning Annex that teaches you how to carry on a conversation or some such nonsense.)

5 Sell Viagra over the Internet. I get so many damn e-mails like that, it must mean *somebody* is making money on all that spam.

6 Open up a lemonade stand. As soon as possible, begin to sell franchises until the things are as abundant as those godforsaken Starbucks. Then do an IPO and cash out ASAP.

7 And finally, the Anna Nicole Plan: Pole dance your way to stardom at your local truck-stop gentlemen's club. Marry absurdly wealthy pre-corpse. Sue as many in-laws as necessary. Biggest appeal of this plan: IQ over 40 not required.

Surviving the Modern Workplace

For those of you not fortunate enough to successfully implement one of the several brilliant plans I've outlined in the previous section, it looks as though you'll need to be prepared to slap on a tie every morning and make that lemming-like slog to work. But before you embark upon this life-long, mind-numbing exercise, allow me to share an abbreviated preview of what you're in for. As a matter of fact, you might just want to tuck it away for future reference in that shabby, unfashionable briefcase you'll be lugging to and fro.

First, there is the commute. This is the part of the day where the slow but gradual wearing away of your very human essence begins. Sure, you may try to deceive your-self into believing that you're "spending the time in the car wisely." Perhaps you multitask by making calls on your cell phone (but, in fact, all you are doing is slowly but surely guaranteeing your local brain surgeon a nice, fat windfall come ten or eleven years from now). Or maybe you pop in that book on tape (but, again, you are rotting your brain, only in a different way . . . you see, this time the weapon of choice is *The Bridges of Madison County*).

So, you finally arrive at the office only to find yourself having to alternatively ask and then answer the terribly probing and provocative question, "Did you have a nice weekend?" forty-seven different times. And let's face it: Despite the fact that most of the replies *should* fall along the lines of, "Well, I spent most of Saturday and Sunday trying to ignore the loveless marriage and spoiled brats I've surrounded myself with while being tranquilized by the narcotic of back-to-back-to-back NFL football in order to keep myself from

Must we make small talk every time we pass?

HOW ABOUT A LITTLE LESS QUESTIONS AND A LITTLE MORE SHUT THE HELL UP?

pondering the very real possibility that I might be gay," the *reality* is that the most interesting reply you're liable to get is, "Well, the wife and I finally caught that new Keanu Reeves movie." Good lord, please shoot me.

About now, the boss starts to send everyone menacing looks, causing you all to scatter to your respective veal pens (commonly known as cubicles). And once there, you spend more time playing FreeCell or trying to *conceal* the fact that you're playing FreeCell than you do putting together that spreadsheet that the marketing people claim to be so breathlessly anticipating. Well, I got news for you, Paco. The marketing department is spending most of *their* time playing Minesweeper, so you've got nothing to worry about.

Janey from accounting (who's far too bubbly not to be an android) swings by about now to drag you into a meeting, the substance of which you really only slightly understand. You sit through it while several people mindlessly toss around buzzwords like "synergy" and "leverage" (all in an attempt to convince the boss that they really *do* know what they're doing and shouldn't be fired for being the frauds that they really are). You suffer through this pointless ritual, hopefully keeping your mouth shut as much as possible, lest it become apparent that you are as clueless as the other drones around the table. Again, you return to your veal pen.

Finally, that clock ticks down to lunchtime and now you've got a whole sixty minutes to scramble out to Chili's and wolf down a plate of Buffalo-somethings before racing back to the office in time to take your postlunch crap and then hustle back to your veal pen before the buzzer sounds. Having fun so far? Then you probably pretend to do a bit more work . . . maybe you kill twenty minutes of the afternoon by wandering over to the kitchenette where Harv from sales chews with his mouth full of stale cheese danish as he recounts to you in excruciating detail how hilarious last night's *Hope & Faith* was because Faith actually had to pretend she was drunk at the church picnic! Ugh. Well, finally, Harv finishes telling you how he laughed milk out his nose and you amble back to the pen for the last tortuous hour and a half of the workday.

Finally, the clock strikes six and you buckle yourself back into that nondescript, midsize American car of yours and plod back home along the interstate, just in time to heat up a frozen dinner and let the incessant cacophony of *The Apprentice* wash over you. But don't stay up too late, old chum, as you'll need to be up at the crack of dawn to repeat this entire exercise in futility and wasted time all over again tomorrow. Happy forty years!

Happy forty years!

Taxes

I'm sure you've heard it many times before . . . The old bit about death and taxes. That's right: Two things that the highest-earning one percent of the country can avoid with the help of the proper legal team. Oh, I kid, of course. That would actually be a jail sentence for murdering your wife I'm thinking of (yes, I'm talking to you, Juice).

Anyhoo, if you think about it, Walt Disney may have had his head frozen, but he still couldn't avoid the taxman, could he? And it has always seemed like such a terribly unjust system to me. Why should we be compelled to hand over so much of our hard-earned moola to that hopelessly inept entity known as the U.S. government? After all, **I'm not running a damn charity over here!**

Now some might say to me, "Fine, Stewart. You don't want to pay taxes? Then you don't get to use the roads. Or the schools. Or blah, or blah, or

> That is freakin' sweet!

blah." Well, imaginary debating opponent, I've got news for you: That suits me just fine. You see, I've always been a fan of homeschooling, anyway (no distractions such as the pressure to find someone to "go steady with"), and I don't need to use your silly roads, either.

In fact, I'd prefer it if we all just blazed our own trails to wherever our busy days took us. Fewer roads equals more traffic. More traffic equals more stress. **More stress equals more mayhem.** And more mayhem equals a power vacuum that provides an opportunity for yours truly to swoop in and conquer the quarreling masses, and finally enslave them to serve me and me alone! And then I can start to charge them taxes. Didn't see that one coming, did you? Ha!

Chapter 8

TV, Entertainment, and Pop Culture, or The Very Few Virtues of the Idiot Box

I'm not sure that I can place the exact moment in time that demarcated the decline of Western Civilization, but it's a safe bet that moment was televised. You see, it's not like the old days, my friends, when the family could all sit contentedly around the RCA, sipping chocolate phosphates and listening to broadcasts from the European front. No, no, no. Now if you even simply want to enjoy the camaraderie and cheap snack foods at your neighborhood Super Bowl party, before you know it, bam! . . . suddenly, you've got the second banana of the Royal Family of Freakishness flinging her bosom at you and the rest of the free world.

The only thing I do know for certain is that when I have my own children there is no chance whatsoever that I will allow them to be subjected to some of the various televised cultural atrocities I've been forced to witness in my own young life (beginning with being constrained at an early age in a Jolly Jumper while the other rocket scientists of clan Griffin got their fill of *Small Wonder*).

So, in these next few pages, I'd like to give you a little heads up or two on some of the worst offenders. (It won't be difficult since the fat man has Season Passes for most of them.) And if possible, I'd like to point out some of the bright spots in the bleak pop culture landscape, as well. After all, I certainly wouldn't ever want to be thought of as someone who was just negative all the time, now would I?

The Local News

They take on different forms in different localities. Some of the specifics may vary from place to place, **but the one televised horror you are almost certain to have foisted upon you regardless of your geography is that daily insipid tripe known as the local news.** I'm sure you are familiar with the whole drill, but for the sake of tradition, allow me to walk you through the typical newscast at Channel 8 or 10 or 3 in every tiny burg and hamlet of these grand United States.

First, we open with the highly self-important and overproduced intro, usually featuring shots of the news team either giving stern contemplative looks of faux gravitas or smarmy "see, I could be your best drinking buddy" grins (this one most often used by the high-school-jock-who-never-made-it sports anchor).

We then cut to the ridiculously coiffed male and female anchors (often of

various ethnicities, of course), who, between moronic banter, manage to squeeze in a few news stories of marginal significance. And God help us all if Captain Bob in News Chopper 12 gets wind of a high-speed chase, because then all bets are off and that's what you're going to be stuck watching for the remainder of the broadcast. Election results? That'll have to wait.

TV, Entertainment, and Pop Culture, or
The Very Few Virtues of the Idiot Box

The Pope died? Don't care. Plane crash? Not as far as we're concerned, because we just heard some two-bit red-light-runner decided he could outrun the local sheriff, despite the fact that every television camera in the county is now pointed directly at him. Yeah, that's some good thinking, old chap. Only thing is, now you're probably going to make me miss *Jeopardy!* too, you putz.

Anyhow, after suffering through the obligatory (and usually not particularly clever) sports

Sorry, kids. Daddy loves you, but Daddy also loves TV, and TV was here first.

bloopers presented by the sportscaster whose first name is probably something synonymous with a rock (if not actually "Rock") as well as all the blue-screen gaffes of the weatherman who really wanted to be a stand-up comedian but couldn't cut it ("Oh, dear! He's wearing a blue tie and so now it looks like he's got scattered rain showers on his beer gut!"), then it's time to get the daily social commentary from the airheaded news anchor summing up what all these zany current events mean to those of us trying to make sense of this crazy modern world in which we live. Well, you know what, Slick? Save your phony empathy, get in your expensive convertible, go cash your fat checks, and get the hell out of my face. I really couldn't care less what you think the teachers' strike at the high school and the overturned truck on the highway mean for the state of society and its prospects for world peace. You make me sick!

And before I leave the topic of local news altogether, I'd simply like to float one tiny question to all those terribly ingenious producers out there: **You know, is there some law requiring that you send the minority reporters to interview the folks in the urban areas?** Do you really believe that people will only feel comfortable responding to a reporter of their own ethnic background? It seems rather sketchy to me, but you know, look, I'm just asking . . . Besides, what do I know, anyway? I'm just a silly baby, right?

Coming up: Diane's weight.

Reality TV

Without a doubt, next on the hit parade of televised crimes against humanity has to be the genre of reality TV.

Now, please don't misunderstand me. **I was right there with you crazy kids during those first heady days of *The Real World.*** Sure, I knew all of it was false, that this group of young people could never actually live in such a palatial domicile, that they could never have the job opportunities, or endure the contrived conflicts that were artificially injected into the show. But fie on being upset that the telly dared to deceive me! I cared not at all, because watching that program meant for a delicious thirty minutes I got to sit back and ogle that shapely vixen Julie.

But, alas, since those innocent days of false pretense and televised stereotypes, we've come to the edge of the pit of Hades, for now we are subjected on a weekly basis to svelte hardbodies eating bugs or pretending to be interested in finding a mate for the sake of garnering their fifteen minutes of fame.

And oh, all the trickery! A young lady lies to a young man about her marital status, *he* lies to *her* about the size of his personal fortune, and we all lie to ourselves that this nonsense isn't rotting the very moral fiber of our society.

But before I start sounding too much like some Baptist preacher you'd find in a tent in rural Kentucky, I must confess that I have no choice but to assign equal blame to both the producers of such schlock, and to the segments of the viewing audience who gravitate toward these programs.

> The stark truth of my situation is that I submitted a tape to be on *Survivor* but they didn't pick me.

Indeed, does it say more about our culture that such programs would be on television in the first place, or that such a large audience would go out of their way to watch?

All right, all right . . . time to really, truly level with you here, dear reader. My anger really doesn't come from any moral high ground. The stark truth of my situation is that I submitted a tape to *Survivor Season 6* and they didn't pick me. To be honest, I realize now that I've never really truly gotten over that. You see, I had a great idea for my submission tape: Rupert and I were going to re-create an old ventriloquism act I'd seen on *The Ed Sullivan Show*. But, no, that drunkard dog told us, "every season they pick someone who sends in a tape of themselves in the nude." And stupid me listened to him and sent in a tape of me riding a tricycle in the buff while singing "The Surrey with the Fringe on Top." And I never even got a reply from the *Survivor* folks. I just wish I could say the same for our local law enforcement. Would you believe the feds actually showed up at the house and put the fat man through the wringer on a whole child pornography interrogation? No, I, I, I felt bad . . . a little.

Damn *Survivor*. Screw them, anyway.

I like you, Mark Burnett . . . When the world is mine, your death shall be quick and painless.

What's Wrong with Television Today

One might understandably assume that I hold nothing but utter disdain for the medium of television. Quite the contrary, in fact. At its best, I actually feel that television has the potential to uplift the human spirit and highlight facets of our collective experience unlike any other of the mass media (my apologies for briefly sounding like an Emmy commentary from that self-important bastard Bryant Gumbel).

Nonetheless, there are areas where television could do better or try harder, and I've highlighted some of those instances below:

1 Everyone's always plugging something. You know, just once I'd like to witness a talk show host having a normal human conversation with a guest. It seems every celebrity appearance has the air of Ben Stiller shamelessly shilling the latest talking picture he's crapped out.

2 Too many copies of the same show. Let me put it to you this way: I understand CBS is planning a *CSI: Duluth*. Enough said.

3 *Extra, Entertainment Tonight,* and *Access Hollywood*. I'm still attempting to assess the exact genre into which this garbage falls. For example, is it *news* to know what Thora Birch happened to say about Bennifer on her way into a movie premiere? I should think not. But then, these train wrecks aren't really *entertainment,* either. Certainly, watching that hyperactive Bush boy document his day riding in the limo of the gentleman who voices virtually every single movie trailer could hardly be characterized as amusing. Sitting through that feels more like something out of *A Clockwork Orange,* I would say, no?

4 **The notion of the airwaves belonging to the public is long since dead.** Please forgive the soapbox for a moment, but there used to be a notion in this country that the airwaves through which television is delivered were actually regarded as a public resource, belonging collectively to each and every taxpayer in the land (and that the networks, as custodians of such, had an obligation to serve the public's interest). However, that concept has been summarily trampled by the unending avarice of the small cartel of companies that now deliver all we read, hear, and know about the world. So, we now have piped into our homes, for instance, an alleged "news" network, which in reality merely functions as a mouthpiece for the Repub— I'm very sorry. It appears that I've just been handed a telegram. Evidently, I've been ordered to cease and desist this conversation and to politely invite you to continue on to the next section of this book. Apparently I terribly regret having troubled you with this last point, and I am supposed to ask that you now strike it from your memory. Thank you so much.

My Advice to Britney, Christina, and Jessica

All right, ladies, listen up. Since each of your fifteen minutes appears to be wrapping up faster than a coked-up elf on Christmas Eve, allow me to offer my thoughts on each of your futures:

- **Britney,** you have such a shining light inside you. I only wish you would realize that you don't need to always go to the sex-well in order to sell records. If I could share with you just one piece of advice, it would be to stop parading around like a two-bit tramp and just let your talent speak for itsel— I'm sorry, I'm sorry, I couldn't even say that with a straight face. No, no, Brit-Brit. Better keep flaunting the goods, girlfriend, 'cause that's about all you're coasting on these days.

- **Christina,** now you're the one my heart truly does go out to. You poor thing, I realize you kissed Madonna at the VMAs, too, yet all anyone could talk about afterward was Britney this, Britney that . . . I swear, if you ever hope to get out of Britney's shadow, it seems you're going to have to dry hump a cross-dressing midget at the Republican National Convention. Hmm . . . wait a moment, now actually, that's not bad. Christina, if you happen to be reading this, please contact my people so we can set up a lunch.

- **Jessica,** best be careful, sweetheart, I see you maimed in a stupidity-related accident sometime around 2011.

Chapter 9

Inventions <Those Actually Operational as Well as Those Still Tied Up in R&D>

As a special treat to you, dear reader, I have compiled a short list of some of the inventions I have been working on as of late. Before you judge them too harshly, though, please be aware that while some have gone all the way to the prototype stage, others remain firmly stuck in Research and Development. But, after all, it's a process, no?

Oh, and by the way, Rupert has suggested that perhaps I was not entirely fair in my earlier comments to both Ozzy Osbourne and Jimmy Fallon and he has strongly advised me to apologize to them both for what I said. So, uh, yeah . . . sorry. There. You happy now, Rupert? Are you happy now that you embarrassed me in front of everyone? You know, you always get neurotic and controlling like this right after we run into my ex–teddy bear at the market. I'm just saying that it would be more emotionally honest of you to— Look, Rupert and I evidently have some issues to discuss here, so please continue on through the chapter without me. Thank you.

What follows is merely a brief sampling of what's been going on in the lab of late (aside from the never-ending droll and witty banter between Rupert and me, of course).

Currently Operational Devices

■ **Energy Converter.** This unit converts the waste material found in a soiled diaper into kilowatts of electrical power. Three months it's been up and running and Lois still thinks I'm just constipated.

■ **Food Concentrator** (for use with broccoli). This one takes broccoli and distills its essence into pill form. Much as I hate to eat the stuff, I'm not foolish enough to pass up the valuable antioxidants it contains.

Inventions in Development

■ **Thought Translator.** This device detects mental activity and then actually translates thoughts into language. However, thus far, the damn thing will only transcribe ideas into Aramaic. I suppose Mel Gibson could have used this one for that three-hour snoozefest he insisted on cramming down America's throat.

■ **BS-o-meter.** When completed, this scanner will be able to intake any written document and generate a numerical rating of the lies and exaggerations contained within. I know this device is close to completion because I recently tested it on an Internet press release I found that was hyping "Quintuplets." The thing started smoking and then blew a fuse.

■ **Smirk Remover.** A machine that would give literal meaning to wiping the smirk off someone's face. Don't try to tell me you wouldn't want one.

Chapter 10

Collected Essays and Journal Entries, or Some Notions I Scribbled on a Napkin While Trapped with the Family at KFC

Tomorrow's forecast: Sprinkle of genius with chance of doom.

What I've Learned from Literature

It's a real tragedy what's happened to literacy in this country of ours. Fact is, I pride myself on the amount of reading I do, but then, as a baby, what else really is there to occupy my days (aside from the obvious diaper filling and matricide)?

So, in light of the era of Cliffs Notes in which we live (honestly, when was the last time the average student today actually read an entire novel?), I've accumulated a short list of some of the important lessons that we can cull from some of the classics.

1 As Poe so succinctly put it, the death of a beautiful woman is, unquestionably, the most poetic subject in the world. Be it Little Nell from Dickens's *The Old Curiosity Shop*, Little Eva from *Uncle Tom's Cabin*, or Poe's very own "The Raven," we see it again and again. Let that serve as a warning shot across your bow, Lois.

2 Originality is overrated (and in the case of Shakespeare, it is evidently not important at all. Do you know that bloody chap stole all but one of his plots? Hmm, apparently, crime *does* pay).

3 Defoe's *Robinson Crusoe* shows us that survival against the elements is difficult, but manageable. An important fact to tuck away for you wanna-be world conquerors out there. Or wanna-be *Survivor* contestants.

4 Complain as you might about public school (as even I did earlier in this tome), both *David Copperfield* and *Jane Eyre* demonstrate that being sent away to school is never, ever a good thing. That is, unless you enjoy hunger, cold, and wicked teachers.

5 And, finally, something to file as a "Note to Self." We see clearly in *Beowulf* that a mother's revenge is swift and powerful. So, then . . . right back at you, Lois, I suppose. Not the worst thing, though, since the best challenge is always a well-matched fight, no? We certainly saw that in *Rocky* as well, hmm?

A Thought or Two on Alcohol

Alcohol. It's certainly the root of many of society's ills. And Lord knows *The Untouchables* would have been much less watchable had it never existed. (Though truth be told, Kevin Costner's wooden acting nearly dealt that flick a death blow right out of the gate, hmm?)

In any case, my experience has been primarily as an observer of someone who regularly uses the substance to numb himself to the tedium of daily life. (Yes, I'm talking about that fleabag with whom I am forced to share a domicile.) Matter of fact, I've only seen the dog totally sober on maybe a handful of occasions. But I can't really criticize the fellow too much since I myself live in a glass house, totally dependent on that bottle of mine. (Much as I've tried to give it up, that damn nipple keeps singing its enticing siren song.)

Still, it's curious to me that a substance that tastes like rat urine, while also inducing vomiting and ill-advised mating, has such a powerful grip on our culture. But, then again, people have always shown a knack for yearning after precisely the things that are worst for them. Exhibit A: the success of Michael Bolton. Frankly, it's all too much to contemplate . . . Aggh, perhaps *I* need a drink!

A MARTINI A DAY
KEEPS THE FLEAS AWAY

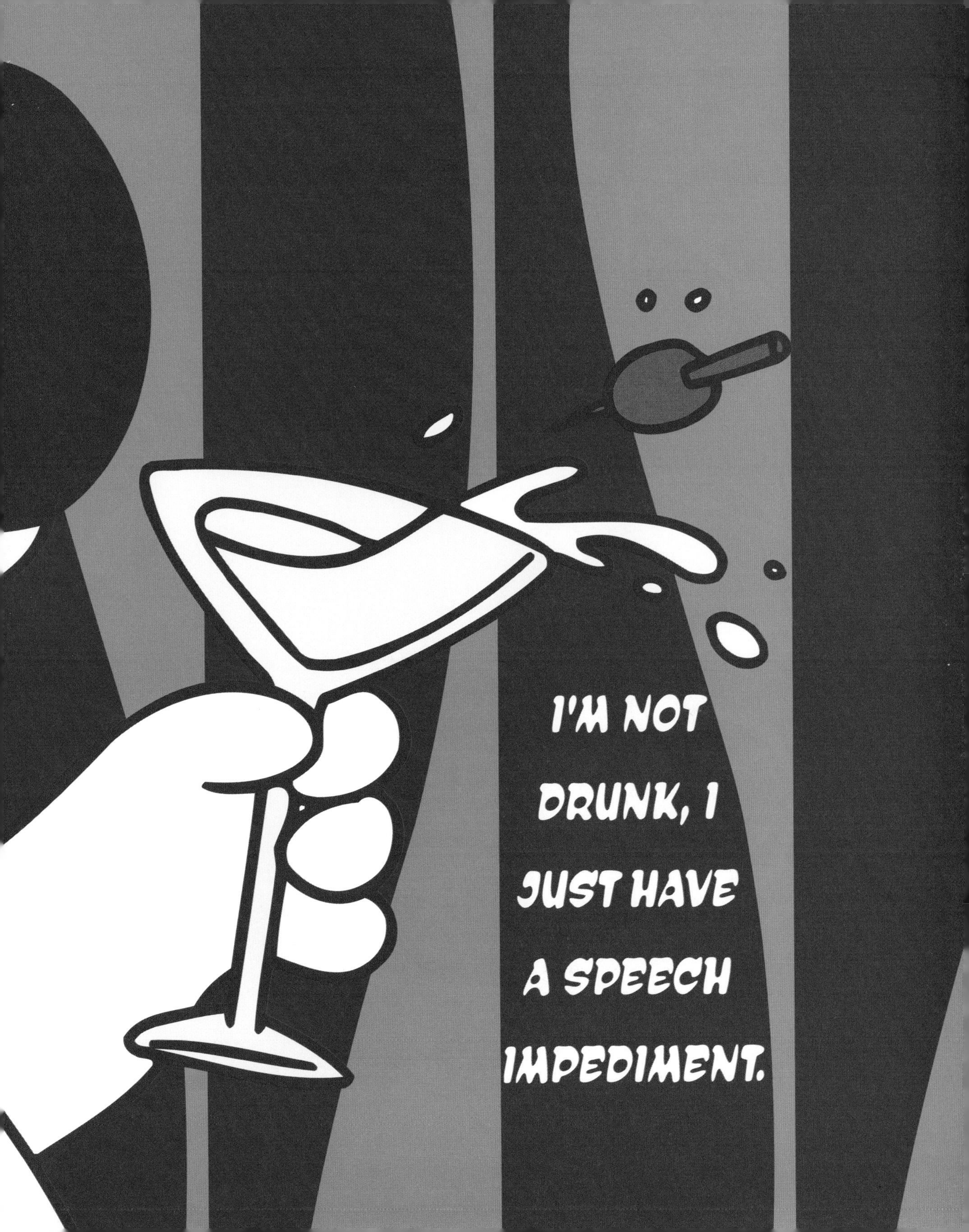
I'M NOT DRUNK, I JUST HAVE A SPEECH IMPEDIMENT.

The Evil Monkey in Chris's Closet

Ah, the monkey in Chris's closet. Is it real? Is it merely a metaphor for Chris's own self-doubt and teen angst? No one knows for sure.

The poor boy mentions it so often and always sounds so terrified; I tried on one occasion to look into it. I snooped around that closet for the better part of an afternoon and I'll tell you that all I managed to dig up were some staggeringly foul-smelling gym clothes and a tattered copy of the Victoria's Secret catalog. I later heard Chris explaining to the fat man that Wednesdays are the monkey's afternoon at the gym. And while I suppose that is a likely alibi, I don't know, I must say I'm not convinced.

I *did* find what appeared to be poop in the far end of the closet, but that could very well have been Chris just not wanting to make the trek down the hall. So, the quest for truth continues, I suppose . . .

A Final Word on World Domination

And so we come to the end of our journey. It is my sincere hope that you were able to extract something of some value from all this rambling. But if nothing else, I would expect that you have a much more thorough understanding of this world and can now spot all the potential footholds from which to unleash your reign of terror.

However, I must caution you not to take the matter of world domination too lightly. As Tobey Maguire said in that overrated piece of schlock, "With great power comes great responsibility." Conquering the masses is the easy part. Keeping them from toppling and then killing you is quite another. And I know what you're thinking: "Just get yourself a good death squad." But I'll tell you right now, your average death squad is not as skilled or as loyal as you'd think they'd be.

So, you've got to stop the uprisings before they even begin. And here's the one big secret of this entire book: It's the toilets, stupid. That's right. The first thing that's going to make oppressed people snap and want to come after their oppressors with the nearest and sharpest stick is not having a relatively clean and private place to do their business. Trust me on this. I know people. And they get positively mental about their doodie. So, if you want to stay in power, first make sure the rest rooms are up to snuff.

All right, then, that's the end of my lesson. So, fly, you mad power-hungry wanna-be dictator, fly. And make old Stewie proud. Oh, and of course . . . burn in hell!

Snippets from Stewie's Press Junket

Just prior to the publication of this book, I was inundated with requests for interviews from the media. Charlie Rose called me, as did Larry King, as well as that multicultural coven from *The View*. Dan Rather even called me personally, however, I had to decline the interview due to his grating and excessive use of "down home"–isms. And just for the record, Dan, I most certainly do not "spew venom like a rattler cornered by the village blacksmith at Grandma's watering hole."

Anyhoo, because I didn't want to run the risk of being as overexposed as Tara Reid's left bosom, I granted an exclusive interview to one paper only, *The Quahog Informant*. Their coverage of the fat man's prior attempts to cede from the union, I thought, was unusually balanced. What follows is an excerpt from that rare interview.

Why did you write this book?

Well, as I tell my minions, true domination can only result from bearing this single truth in mind: *The key to world domination is* understanding *the world around you.* Hence this weighty tome serves as a sort of guide toward that end. And besides, I figured Bill Clinton didn't do too shabbily with his book. I mean, come on, that thing read like a giant brain dump transcribed from doodled-on legal pads and soiled cocktail napkins, and he certainly cashed in.

Having completed it with this purpose in mind, are you any closer to achieving complete enlightenment and thus world domination?

World domination is right around the corner for me. Just as soon as I can get my laptop and my PDA networked. I have an IT guy coming to look at it, but he keeps rescheduling on me. And regarding enlightenment, I try to get myself to yoga twice a week. It gives me a feeling of calm and centeredness while allowing me to scope out some of the neighborhood MILFs.

Just about every kid thinks he's adopted at some point in his life. And it's no secret that you are very different from the other members of your family. Genetically speaking, where do you suppose you get your unique brand of genius?

Having been incarcerated in her vile womb for nine months, I can say with certainty that the wretched nasally voiced redhead is my mother, but one glance at the fat man tells you I'm hardly a chip off the old moron. So, let's just say I wouldn't be surprised if you were to tell me the milkman has an enormous, football-shaped head.

If you could choose to join any other family in history, what family would that be?

Dr. Phil's. Not because I think it'd be smooth sailing, mind you. You know, what if the guy's life is really a complete train wreck. Imagine the perverted pleasure I'd get observing the irony of someone like that lining his pockets by shouting inane aphorisms to white trash couples on national television.

You take television (and pop culture in general) to task in this book. If you had your own show, what would it be like?

One part *Sonny and Cher*. One part *Hawaii Five-0*. Three parts *Benny Hill*. However, I'm certain that such a show would inevitably get jostled around into six or seven time slots over a year and a half's time, only to be ruthlessly canceled by the powers-that-be, whereupon I would have no choice but to command my loyal masses to lead a revolt to get the program reinstated on the airwaves. Or something like that, I don't know. . . .

You also criticize the school system heavily in your book. If there was one mandatory thing in classrooms everywhere, what do you think that should be?

Body armor.

You write extensively about young people today and some about the stresses of being a baby, too. If you could remain one age for all of life, what age would that be?

Two. By then you're tall enough to reach most things around the house, and I would assume people would take you a bit more seriously than when you were only one. However, you're still young enough to get away with having other people demean themselves by changing your back-loaded diapers.

You also talk a good deal about the sexes in this book. You actually sound as if you are talking from personal experience. Have you ever been in love before?

Well, fans of the show would know that I was briefly in love with a harlot named Janet before I realized she was only using me for my cookies. And there was one other love in my life, but pending legal action prevents me from discussing her publicly . . . or coming within two hundred yards of her.

You wax on about what you've learned from literature. What do you hope readers will learn from your book?

That while you can't choose the family you're born into, you can choose which method of enslaving them will prove most amusing to you.

Fashion horrors are also a favorite topic in the book. You dress down several people for their poor sartorial judgment. But is there anyone you think consistently dresses to kill, as they say?

Of course, Ted Bundy always did. I'm sorry, but even you have to admit you totally set me up for that. On a serious note, though, I must say that, naysayers be damned, I always thought Bjork nailed it.

Not even the local news escaped your sharp tongue. If you were ever to make the evening news, what would you hope it would be for?

I'm tempted to say "making the bestseller list," but the honest answer is that I've always wanted to be featured in the sports roundup footage as one of those quirky fans who cleverly uses the acronym of the network that aired the game and then posts it on a giant poster. You know, like, "Can't Beat the Seahawks." That always tickles me. Of course, I don't particularly like the Seahawks. . . . In fact, I've never even been to Seattle, but, you know, you see my point.

You cover a hell of a lot more than just these topics in your book, but two I have not yet mentioned, though I think they are particularly interesting coming from a toddler, are the chapters on work and taxes. If you got a whopping tax refund . . . or a lot of money in royalties, what would you spend that money on?

Weapons-grade plutonium, a manual on interrogation techniques, and a hoppity horse.

OFFICIAL RULES

1. NO PURCHASE OR PAYMENT NECESSARY TO ENTER OR WIN.

2. **How to Enter.** To enter, complete the official entry form or hand print your name, address, age, and phone number along with the words "Family Guy: Stewie's Guide to World Domination Sweepstakes" on a 3" x 5" card and mail to: Family Guy: Stewie's Guide to World Domination Sweepstakes, c/o HarperEntertainment, Attn: Marketing Department, 10 East 53rd Street, New York, NY 10022. Entries must be received no later than September 30, 2005. Enter as often as you wish, but each entry must be mailed separately. One entry per envelope. Partially completed, illegible, or mechanically reproduced entries will not be accepted. Entries which are otherwise not in compliance with these Official Rules will also be disqualified. Sponsor is not responsible for lost, late, mutilated, illegible, stolen, postage due, incomplete, or misdirected entries. All entries become the property of Twentieth Century Fox, and will not be returned.

3. **Eligibility.** Sweepstakes open to all legal residents of the United States (excluding Colorado and Rhode Island), excluding employees and immediate family members of HarperCollins Publishers, Inc., ("HarperCollins"), Twentieth Century Fox ("Fox"), Fuzzy Door Productions and their respective subsidiaries and affiliates, officers, directors, shareholders, employees, agents, attorneys, advertising, promotion and fulfillment agencies and other representatives and their immediate families. All applicable federal, state and local laws and regulations apply. Offer void where prohibited or restricted by law.

4. **Odds of Winning.** Odds of winning depend on the total number of entries received. Approximately 50,000 sweepstakes announcements published. All prizes will be awarded. Winner will be randomly drawn on or about November 15, 2005, by HarperCollins, whose decision is final. Potential winner will be notified by mail and will be required to sign and return an affidavit of eligibility and release of liability within 14 days of notification. If a potential winner cannot be reached after a reasonable effort has been exerted or if s/he is found to be ineligible or if s/he cannot or does not comply with these Official Rules, an alternate winner may be selected. Failure to sign and return an affidavit of eligibility and release of liability within 14 days of notification, or return of prize or prize notification as undeliverable, will result in disqualification of the winner and an alternate winner will be selected. Prizes won by minors will be awarded to parent or legal guardian who must sign and return all required legal documents. By acceptance of their prize, winners consent to the use of their names, photographs, likeness, biographical information and his/her address (limited to city and state) by HarperCollins and Twentieth Century Fox, and for publicity purposes without further compensation worldwide and in perpetuity in any and all forms of media, now known and hereafter devised, including without limitation the Internet, unless prohibited by law.

5. **Grand Prize.** One **Grand Prize Winner** will win one original *Family Guy* drawing. Approximate retail value of prize totals $200.00.

6. **Prize Limitations.** All prizes will be awarded. Only one prize will be awarded per individual, family, or household. Prizes are non-transferable and cannot be sold or redeemed for cash. No cash substitute is available. Any federal, state, or local taxes are the responsibility of the winner. Sponsor may substitute prize of equal or greater value, if necessary, due to availability.

7. **Additional terms:** By participating, entrants agree a) to the official rules and decisions of the judges, which will be final in all respects; and to waive any claim to ambiguity of the official rules and b) to release, discharge, and hold harmless HarperCollins, Twentieth Century Fox, and Fuzzy Door Productions and their respective parent companies, affiliates, subsidiaries, employees and representatives and advertising, promotion and fulfillment agencies from and against any and all liability or damages associated with acceptance, use, or misuse of any prize received or participation in any Sweepstakes-related activity or participation in this Sweepstakes.

8. **Dispute Resolution.** Any dispute arising from this Sweepstakes will be determined according to the laws of the State of New York, without reference to its conflict of law principles, and the entrants consent to the personal jurisdiction of the State and Federal courts located in New York County and agree that such courts have exclusive jurisdiction over all such disputes.

9. **Winner Information.** To obtain the name of the winner, please send your request and a self-addressed stamped envelope (residents of Vermont may omit return postage) to Family Guy Original Drawing Sweepstakes Winner, c/o HarperEntertainment, 10 East 53rd Street, New York, NY 10022 after January 1, 2006, but no later than June 1, 2006.

10. **Sweepstakes Sponsor:** HarperCollins Publishers.

 # Original Drawing Sweepstakes

Enter to win a one-of-a-kind original production drawing from the hit television show *Family Guy*, which features a fearless Stewie Griffin dressed as the intractable conqueror Napoleon Bonaparte. This illustration at once calls attention to Stewie's diminutive stature while also reminding fans of his enormous ambition to conquer the world!

Don't miss *Family Guy: The Ultimate Episode Guide* coming in Fall 2005! To receive notice of author events and new *Family Guy* books by Steve Callaghan, sign up at www.authortracker.com.

Mail to: *Family Guy: Stewie's Guide to World Domination* Sweepstakes
c/o HarperEntertainment
Attn: Marketing Department
10 East 53rd Street
New York, New York 10022

Name: _____

Address: _____

City: _____ State: _____ Zip: _____

Phone: _____

No purchase necessary.

Perennial Currents
An Imprint of HarperCollinsPublishers

FOX

FAMILY GUY

Acknowledgments

This book would not have been possible without the guidance of Debbie Olshan and the patience, diligence, and creativity of Hope Innelli. In addition, the countless insights into the mother-toddler relationship at the very core of this book flow solely and directly from Quinn, the joyful and loving toddler who fills my own life with happiness on a daily basis, as well as from Phyllis, the truly remarkable mother with whom I spent years that were thoroughly wonderful and yet far too few in number. And, finally, this book would not even exist (quite literally so) if not for Seth MacFarlane to whom I am enormously grateful for his friendship, his generosity, and his extraordinary comedic talents.

—S.C.

And, of course, it wouldn't be possible without me either.

—S.G.